The Camp Fire Mystery

THE BOBBSEY TWINS®

THE
CAMP FIRE
MYSTERY

Laura Lee Hope

Illustrated by John Speirs

WANDERER BOOKS
Published by
Simon & Schuster, New York

Manufactured in the United States of America
10 9 8 7 6 5 4 3 2

WANDERER and colophon are trademarks of Simon & Schuster

THE BOBBSEY TWINS is a trademark of Stratemeyer Syndicate,
registered in the United States Patent and Trademark Office

Library of Congress Cataloging in Publication Data
Hope, Laura Lee.
The camp fire mystery.
(The Bobbsey twins; 6)
SUMMARY: The Bobbsey twins help the members of a Camp Fire
club catch the culprits who stole their bicycles.
[1. Mystery and detective stories. 2. Camping—Fiction] I. Speirs, John,
ill. II. Title. III. Series: Hope, Laura Lee. Bobbsey twins (1980-   ); 6.
PZ7.H772Cam   [Fic]   81-24090
ISBN 0-671-43374-1   AACR2
ISBN 0-671-43373-3 (pbk.)

Contents

The Bobbsey Twins began their adventures in 1904, six years before the founding of Camp Fire in 1910. It isn't hard to imagine the girls and boys of that era, perhaps seated around a campfire, reading about Nan and Bert and Freddie and Flossie. Since then, millions of Camp Fire members have grown up enjoying both the twins and their mysteries.

However, *this* book has special meaning for today's boys and girls—as the Bobbseys join them in Camp Fire. When you think about it, it's not surprising that Camp Fire and the Bobbsey Twins have finally gotten together in this keepsake edition of *The Camp Fire Mystery*. After all, we share a concern about young people and what they can do to make the world a better place for themselves and for those around them.

And if that happens to involve friends and fun and a little bit of mystery, so much the better!

Roberta van der Voort, Ed. D.
National Executive Director, Camp Fire, Inc.

Often, when we think of those people and organizations who carry on the great traditions of America, we think of Camp Fire and the exciting opportunities it offers boys and girls to learn about themselves and the world they live in.

No wonder, then, it seemed so natural to blend Camp Fire activities into a Bobbsey Twins adventure. In *The Camp Fire Mystery*, the young detectives not only solve a puzzling case or two, but they also acquire new skills and insights. They are taught, for instance, how to construct a bluebird nesting box as part of Camp Fire's project to save the bluebirds. But equally important, they make new, permanent friendships as long-lasting as this special edition meant only for you.

Laura Lee Hope

The author gratefully acknowledges Camp Fire, Inc. and all those who share in its outstanding work for their kind and generous assistance in the preparation of this story.

· 1 ·

The Ghost Balloon

"Look, Freddie!" Flossie Bobbsey cried, pointing her chubby finger at the sky.

She leaped excitedly out of the shade of the adobe house into the early morning sunlight.

"I don't see anything," her six-year-old twin Freddie said with a loud yawn.

He shut his eyes tightly for several seconds before opening them again. Then he saw it, too. An enormous balloon with a circle of pretty bluebirds on it was floating high overhead.

"There's nobody in the balloon basket," Freddie observed as the giant ball drifted lower.

"Maybe a ghost is flying it," his sister said and gulped nervously, "and what if it falls down on top of us?"

"What do you mean by *if*?" Freddie said as the older Bobbsey twins, Nan and Bert, appeared in the doorway of the Leonards' home where they were staying.

"What's all the commotion about?" Nan asked. When she saw the balloon, her eyes opened wide. "It's coming down!" she gasped.

Indeed, the balloon was dropping fast.

"It looks like it's going to crash in the ditch!" Bert shouted, now drawing Mr. and Mrs. Leonard outside.

Kathy Leonard, a college friend of Mrs. Bobbsey's, was a tall, attractive young woman whose blond hair was cut short and tucked behind her ears. Ever since the children had arrived here in New Mexico, she had teased Freddie and Flossie about their blond curls. Couldn't they grow a few extra ones for her? she asked. But at this particular moment, her usually cheerful face was frowning like her husband's.

"I'll call the police," Kathy announced while Tony Leonard raced down the driveway.

"C'mon!" Bert told the other twins and ran after him toward the spot where the balloon seemed headed for a landing.

It barely missed the tops of two trees as it looped toward a bank of weeds and hit the irrigation ditch behind the Leonard home. The deep wicker basket to which the balloon was attached rocked and bounced as the balloon dragged it through the ditch, splattering mud and water everywhere.

"Help! Help!" a man's voice called

out above the barking of a dog.

"That's no ghost! Someone's hurt!" Freddie declared.

"And there's a collie with him!" Nan exclaimed, pointing to the long furry snout that bobbed into view. "Come on!"

At the same time, the balloonist's arm rose over the edge of the basket and tugged on a rope that opened the vent overhead.

"He's letting the air out," Bert said as everyone ran toward it.

"You kids hold down the basket while I help him out," Mr. Leonard said.

"Okay, Mr. Leonard. I mean, Tony," Bert replied, remembering that the couple had asked the children to call them by their first names.

As the man put his hands under the pilot's arms, the dog began to whimper. "You're next, old boy," Tony Leonard told the collie.

The balloonist, who seemed to be in

his thirties, pushed himself forward.

"Can you make it?" Bert asked him.

"I think so," he answered in a voice barely above a whisper.

"Hang on tight, everybody," Nan said. She and the children gripped the sides of the basket.

The balloon was still more than half full of air and, under ordinary circumstances, it could easily have lifted off the ground again. But the nylon frame lay trapped among the weeds and branches. The basket itself was stuck in the mud but had turned over just enough for the collie to leap out as his master kicked free of it.

"What happened?" Flossie asked him when they were on the other side of the ditch.

"I guess I fainted," the young man replied, gingerly touching the fresh scratch on his head.

"You probably hit your head on one of those tanks when you fell," Mr. Leonard observed, motioning toward the heavy metal containers of propane gas at each end of the basket.

Before the pilot had a chance to thank his rescuers, a police car and ambulance pulled into the Leonard's driveway.

"I don't need to go to the hospital," the balloonist murmured.

"But what if you have a concussion?" Bert asked as two policemen raced toward them.

"I'll take my chances that I don't. I have a balloon meet tomorrow, for one thing, and I can't disappoint the club. No, my boy, all I need is a good night's sleep. That's all Lady and I need, don't we, girl?"

The pilot bent down to pet the collie who was nuzzling his leg while one of the uniformed officers asked to see his identification.

"Do you fly for the fun of it?" the policeman asked, examining the driver's license and other cards that the balloonist handed him. "Ryan Michaels—hmm—seems to me I've seen that name around somewhere," the officer went on.

"Maybe in the newspaper. I came in second in last week's balloon race, and there was a write-up about it. And yes, I do fly for the fun of it, officer."

"Well, you better be more careful in the future," the man warned, glancing at the heap of balloon beyond them. "Just what did happen?"

"Air started leaking out and I was forced to land. It's as simple as that."

The young detectives did not interrupt, but they suspected otherwise. They had not seen the pilot standing in the basket when the balloon was in the air. Apparently he had passed out on the floor before he landed, but for some reason, he had decided not to tell the police.

The twins refrained from asking any questions in front of the officers, but they were determined to find out more. When Kathy Leonard offered to give Ryan a cup of tea before he left, the children hoped they would have a chance, but to their disappointment, he declined.

"Lady and I have to go now," he said. "But I'll be back later to pick up the balloon. And thanks again." His eyes fastened gratefully on the children.

"Oh, you're welcome," Bert said. When the man was gone, he asked the Leonards if the twins could look at the balloon again.

"I suppose there's no harm in that," Kathy said. "Go ahead."

Instantly, the children sprinted outside toward the ditch where the balloon and basket lay still in the growing heat of the desert sun.

"You know, even if it were full of air, that balloon couldn't fly now," Bert stated with authority.

"Why not?" Flossie inquired.

"Because the air inside the balloon has to be hotter than outside. The gas in those tanks heats up the inside air and makes the balloon rise, and it can't rise if the outside air is hot, too."

"Thank you very much, Mr. Hot-Air Balloon Expert." Nan said and laughed.

She crunched through the weeds toward the top of the balloon. There were several tears in the nylon, she discovered, but nothing serious. Then her gaze rested near the air vent.

"Come here, everybody!" she cried, pointing to a deep, ragged split in the material.

"It looks like somebody cut right through it with a knife or scissors," Bert said.

On further examination, the four detectives also found a leak in one of the propane gas tanks. Had it occurred when the basket struck the ditch or had someone deliberately punctured the tank? Was it the escaping gas that had made the young balloonist faint?

"But if that's so, then I wonder why Lady didn't pass out, too," Flossie said.

"Maybe she never got close enough to the leak," her twin replied. "Ryan could've been trying to fix the tank when he took a big whiff and fell next to it."

"Well?" Kathy asked the children when they returned to the house. "Did you find out something mysterious?" There was a glint of laughter in her face as she spoke. "Your parents told us to be prepared for trouble when you kids arrived!" she teased.

"Mm-hmm," Freddie said, prompting the older twins to explain what they had found.

The young woman thought about their discovery only a second before saying, "I'm sure there's a perfectly reasonable explanation for everything. We'll ask Mr. Michaels."

"Oh, no," Nan said. "We shouldn't do

that—at least, not right away. I'd like to find out more about him first."

Kathy buried her smile in a soft frown. "I really think you should tell him what you discovered," she said.

"We can't," Flossie insisted.

The young woman, however, was determined to get things out in the open. When Ryan appeared later that afternoon without his collie, she informed him that the twins had a few questions for him.

"What kind of questions? Something about ballooning? Albuquerque's the balloon capital of the world, you know," the pilot said.

"That's very interesting," Bert replied. "Actually—"

"Actually, the children noticed a rip in your balloon, Mr. Michaels," Kathy interjected, much to Bert's chagrin.

"Well—uh, the material's probably worn out around the vent. I'll have to sew it up."

"But it doesn't look worn out," Nan hastened to add.

"Look, I appreciate all you did for me, but my business is my business. Understand?" the balloonist snapped, causing Mrs. Leonard to lift her eyebrows.

"There's no need to raise your voice to these children," she said. "They mean no harm."

As she spoke, they noticed two other men step out of Ryan's pickup truck. Both were of medium build and had stringy blond hair that hung loose around their faces.

They look mean, Nan thought.

The younger twins, meanwhile, had their eyes glued on the back of the truck where awninglike material lay stretched over something.

"Well, I'm going to pack up now," the balloonist said. "Here, take this."

He handed Kathy a few dollar bills.

"What's this for?" she asked.

"For your trouble. Just forget that all of this happened, okay? Buy something for the kids."

Kathy put the money back in Ryan's hand. "We're just glad you weren't injured," she said pleasantly.

"Yeah, yeah," the young pilot said in embarrassment and strode out the door.

"He sure seems nervous about something," Kathy commented.

"You can say that again," Bert said.

The twins went to the kitchen window to watch the men repack the balloon into a big blue bag. But while Ryan was still a number of yards away from his helpers, one of them pointed to the rip.

He said something to his partner, which the children couldn't hear. But the expression on his face was unmistakable. He was worried!

·2·

Bicycle Suspects

Everyone continued to watch the men, unaware that Freddie had ducked outside. He darted toward the truck to get a closer look at it.

I wonder what's under that canvas, the little boy thought.

But before he could investigate, the sound of the men's voices drew nearer, and he sprang behind a nearby yucca plant.

"It's lucky you didn't wind up in the hospital today," one of the stringy-haired men said to Ryan.

"You're not kidding, especially since

I'm in that balloon meet tomorrow," he replied, and stepped into the driver's seat. His assistants dragged the basket and big canvas sack onto the truck.

"Now things are really fouled up," one of them said to the other in a hoarse whisper. "He wants to fly tomorrow and we've got to go to Santa Fe and Pecos to deliver the stuff. How are we going to do it?"

"I don't know. We'll see."

Freddie's heart beat like a tom-tom.

There was something suspicious about the men and he didn't want to be caught listening. Fearfully, he held his breath for several seconds while the men shut the back of the truck. Then he heard the Leonards' front door open.

"Freddie?" Flossie called. "Where are you?"

The little boy did not budge. He knew any slight movement would give away his hiding place, and he was hoping the two men would reveal more.

"Freddie, are you out there?" It was Nan's voice now.

She, Bert, and Flossie were standing in the front yard. They asked the men if they had seen their brother anywhere, which made Freddie cringe even more. He kept wishing they would go away before they found him.

Then, as if they had heard him, the other twins went back inside, allowing him to finish eavesdropping. The men whispered something which he couldn't hear, but after a few seconds their voices grew louder.

"Nice kids, aren't they?" one of the men said.

"Yeah, real nice," his companion replied, leaping off the truck and hooking the latches. "You stay with the balloon and I'll sit up front. Okay?"

"Anything you say, good buddy."

Freddie waited until they were completely out of sight before he stepped out from his hiding place. By now, the sun had settled over the mountains in the distance, turning them deep purple, and a soft wind tossed through the boy's curly hair.

What did the men mean about things being fouled up? he wondered and ran into the house.

"Flossie! Nan!" he cried, bringing them and Bert out of the kitchen.

"Where have you been?" his older brother asked.

Freddie repeated every word he had overheard while his listeners sat with puzzled expressions on their faces.

"It sounds like Ryan's balloon meet could interfere with the other men's plans," Bert said. "And I'd sure like to know what those plans are. What stuff are they delivering and to whom?"

In the meantime, Nan had glanced at the evening edition of the local newspaper, which had just arrived. There was an announcement about the balloon meet that was scheduled to take place

twenty miles east of Santa Fe on the following day.

"This must be the same balloon meet that Ryan was talking about," she said, "and if that's the case . . ."

Her words trailed off, though, as she noticed another headline on the opposite page. It said BICYCLES DISAPPEAR MYSTERIOUSLY.

"Were they stolen?" Flossie inquired, gazing at the newsprint.

"Apparently," Bert replied as he looked over Nan's shoulder. "A whole bunch of them were taken from a camp that's run by the local Camp Fire council here in Albuquerque."

"I'll bet some of the Camp Fire members were starting a bike trip from there," his sister concluded.

"How many bicycles are missing?" Freddie asked.

"At least fifteen."

Kathy and Tony Leonard, who had listened to the children's chatter, grinned at each other. "Do I see the beginnings of a search?" Tony said, laughing.

"Maybe," Nan said. "It's too bad it's so late."

"I agree," Bert chimed in. "I'd like to visit the Camp Fire office."

"You can start your investigation first thing tomorrow morning," Kathy said. "Tonight we have a special treat for you."

"You do?" Flossie asked excitedly.

"That's right," Tony said with a mysterious grin. "Now go change your clothes and be ready to leave as soon as possible."

The twins raced to their rooms and fifteen minutes later were seated in the Leonards' station wagon. It purred through the city streets, leaving the heart of the business district for a long stretch of dusty road that climbed steeply to a parking lot.

"Where are we?" Freddie asked his twin sister.

"I don't know," Flossie whispered back.

The older children, however, had spied the sign marked AERIAL TRAM-WAY and felt a chill of anticipation as everyone hurried up a flight of steps to the boarding platform.

"We're about to take a ride on the world's longest tramway," Kathy announced as the gate opened to admit the group.

The tram itself looked like a giant red box. It was octagonal in shape and had windows all around it.

"All set?" Tony asked as the twins huddled near the front.

"We are," Bert and Nan said enthusiastically. They gazed up at the heavy steel pulleys on which the tram was suspended and waited for the first movement forward.

Freddie and Flossie, too, remained quiet until the tram slid free of the track.

"There's nothing under us now," the little girl exclaimed as Tony lifted her for a better view.

"Of course, there is, honey," Kathy said, smiling. "There are beautiful canyons and trees and—"

"Bighorn sheep!" Nan cried, spotting the great curved horns of one leaping onto a rocky ledge.

"But he doesn't have any wool," Freddie commented as he stood on tiptoe.

"That's right, he doesn't," Kathy said. "He really looks more like a deer."

The tram swung past the sheer outcropping and climbed higher and higher over the boulders and trees until the platform at the top emerged in the twilight. Then it slowed, and for a split second Bert's eyes focused on a narrow footpath below.

He wasn't absolutely positive, but he thought that he saw the balloon pilot Ryan Michaels! Bert tugged on Nan's arm and pointed, causing her to squeeze

forward between the younger twins.

"What am I supposed to be looking at?" she asked in bewilderment.

"Ryan Michaels," her brother responded in a low, hushed voice that did not go unheard by the others.

They all peered below intently, but the man had already disappeared into the shadows of the trees.

"How far did we ride?" the older Bobbsey boy asked the Leonards.

"About two and a half miles," Tony said, "and now we're 10,000 feet over Albuquerque."

"I'll bet that Ryan came up here right after he left us."

"Why do you say that?" Freddie asked.

"Well, for one thing, it's a pretty long trip and he would need sunlight to hike around down there. Or maybe it wasn't Ryan, after all," Kathy said. "Maybe it was someone else or just a spooky shadow."

"Like the ghost who flew the balloon?" Flossie giggled, causing a flush of red to creep up Bert's neck.

"You'll see," he said confidently.

When the passengers debarked, they headed for the restaurant nestled at the peak's edge. The remaining sunlight poured through the window, blanketing their table, and Bert asked to be excused for a moment.

He darted toward the open door that led to the observation deck and scanned the immediate vicinity. Ryan was nowhere in sight, but the young detective waited patiently. He was sure the falling darkness would force the balloonist to come out of the woods!

·3·

False Report

As Bert stood gazing at the rocky panorama that spread red and purple before him, he kept his eyes on the walkway that led from the restaurant.

The sound of his sister's voice, however, made him return inside. "Dinner's on the table," Nan told him.

"I'm coming," Bert said, clearly disappointed to leave his observation post.

"Is Ryan gone?" Freddie asked.

"I guess so," Bert replied. He nibbled at his string beans.

"Cheer up, son," Tony Leonard said, buttering a fresh roll. "Maybe you'll have better luck tomorrow."

Next morning, the young detectives woke up early. They helped Kathy water the garden while it was still cool. Then they devoured a platter of scrambled eggs and bacon.

"Would you mind taking us to the Camp Fire office?" Bert asked Kathy.

"It's number one on my list of things to do today," she said brightly. "By the way, I just received a letter from your parents. They'll be coming here on Monday."

"Oh, goody!" Flossie exclaimed cheerfully.

At the moment, Mr. and Mrs. Bobbsey were attending a national convention for their service club in Chicago. The children had traveled with them that far, then caught a connecting flight to Albuquerque where Kathy picked them up.

"Maybe you'll have solved a mystery or two by then," the young woman said, winking.

To her amazement, the local Camp

Fire council executive director was not only elated but somehow relieved to meet the twin detectives.

"My name is Narosonia Spatz," the woman said after Kathy and the children introduced themselves.

She had sparkling blue eyes that seemed to dance when Bert said they'd like to help find the missing bicycles.

"You know, I've read about your detective work in the newspaper. I can't wait for our Blue Birds and Adventurers to meet you all. Blue Birds are the youngest members of our Camp Fire group and Adventurers are our next youngest."

"I imagine that some of the bicycles that were stolen belong to them," Nan said.

"Not some—all." Mrs. Spatz explained what had happened. "The newspaper didn't quite get the whole story, though. You see, there were two thefts, actually."

"Two?" Freddie asked, surprised.

"That's right. The first one occurred up at camp—" the woman began.

"The paper didn't say where your camp is. Is it nearby?" Bert broke in.

"No, no. It's just outside Cuba—west of Santa Fe." She paused briefly. "Anyway, the children had taken their bikes to camp and apparently left them parked outside the dining hall. Next morning, they were all gone."

"This happened last weekend, right?" Nan questioned.

"Right. And the second theft occurred just the other morning—practically in front of my very own eyes, if you can imagine such a thing," the council director went on. "Millie Jefferson—she's one of our club leaders—asked the boys and girls to be here at ten o'clock to start a short bike trip through the Sandia Mountains. A few of the children arrived early so they came into the office to wait. Then—poof—before we knew it, all of those bikes were gone."

"Then those weren't the same kids who lost their bikes at camp, were they?" Bert asked.

"As a matter of fact, they were. When I told old Mr. Staley about the trouble up at camp, he offered to give the children some bikes to use until they found their own."

"Who's Mr. Staley?" Freddie inquired.

"Oh, he's a very nice man who runs a bicycle shop in town," Mrs. Spatz answered sadly. "I felt terrible about telling him that his bikes were stolen as well."

"But it wasn't your fault," Nan said in a comforting voice.

"I know. Still, I feel responsible because I borrowed the bikes."

"Do you suppose we could meet the kids who were here the other morning?" the young detective asked eagerly.

"I was just about to make the same

suggestion," Mrs. Spatz said. "They're planning an overnight camping trip this weekend. Perhaps you'd all like to come along."

"Oh, we'd love to!" the children chorused.

"Okay, then. Let me make a call."

She disappeared into her office and after a few seconds, the twins heard the woman's voice again. "Yes, Millie, isn't it wonderful? I just know they're going to help us get those bikes back!"

The young detectives gulped. Mrs. Spatz was counting on them to solve the mystery. Now, more than ever, they had to!

"It seems to me you Bobbseys have quite a reputation around here," Kathy said. Freddie's face froze in a limp smile.

"What if we don't find them?" he whispered to his sister.

"We will," Flossie said confidently. "We—"

Before she could finish speaking, a

police siren began to blare down the street. It grew louder and louder.

"That police car is coming here!" Freddie exclaimed as the vehicle pulled to a halt outside the front door.

Two officers emerged and strode inside.

"Are you in charge, ma'am?" one of the men asked Kathy.

"No," she said, "Mrs. Spatz is." She pointed to the woman in the back office who was still on the phone. But she hung up when she saw the policemen.

"What can I do for you?" the council director asked them, as she emerged from the back room.

"Someone reported a burglary here," the taller of the two men replied. He wore his cap forward, hiding a very sunburned face.

"Well, I did the other day but—"

"We just stopped in to make a follow-up check. Are you all Camp Fire members?"

"No, the twins are visiting with me and my husband," Kathy replied.

"So you weren't the kids who lost their bikes the other day?" the second policeman asked the children.

"No, and they weren't lost, officer. They were stolen," Nan corrected.

"And we're going to help find them!" Flossie declared. "We're detectives, you know."

"No, we didn't know," the policeman said, giving his companion a sidelong glance. "Have you solved lots of cases like this one?"

"Oh, lots!" Freddie exclaimed.

"I see. Hmm." The man paused. "And did Mrs. Spatz give you the same report she gave headquarters?"

The twins looked at the woman for an answer. "I told them pretty much everything, but of course, I could've forgotten something," the council director said. "Do you happen to have a copy of my report handy?"

The officer shuffled back on his heels. "Uh, no, but I wouldn't worry about it. I mean, I'm sure you didn't forget anything, ma'am," he said. "Is everything else okay here?"

"Yes, fine, officer.

"Well, that's all we wanted to know. Come on, Joe. Let's go."

The pair stepped out the door as quickly as they had entered, leaving the twins somewhat mystified.

"Now what was that about?" Bert asked.

"They're just weird, that's all," Nan remarked, watching the police car roll onto the street again.

"Well, let's not trouble ourselves over them," the council director said and dismissed the subject immediately. "By the way, I was mistaken about the length of the camping trip. I thought it was only one night but it's two. Can you still go?"

"Oh, yes!" the younger twins exclaimed gleefully.

Bert had hoped to revisit Sandia Peak but, seeing Nan's eagerness, agreed to wait until after their return.

"Millie Jefferson will tell you what you need to bring. You can ride up in her car," Mrs. Spatz told the twins. "How does that sound to everybody? Mrs. Leonard?"

"It sounds fine to me," Kathy said while her eyes traveled to a shelf of Camp Fire emblems and a small box of iron-on decals. "These will look great on your T-shirts," she said to the children and purchased four of the iron-ons. Two bore the Camp Fire emblem and the others said "Blue Birds Have Fun."

"I have another idea, too," Mrs. Spatz said, pulling out a box of Camp Fire outfits. "I just happen to have some extra jeans and vests for all of you. Now, if you're about to become members of

Camp Fire, you'll have to dress like them." She handed out the clothes, including a bolo tie for Freddie, which also carried the Camp Fire insignia.

"Oh, thank you," the little boy said, looping the heavy blue braid between his fingers.

On the way home, the children talked about what they had to do—a phone call to Millie Jefferson, then laundry and packing!

Bert's mind was still on Ryan Michaels, though, and his mysterious appearance along the Sandia hiking trail. Unfortunately, there was no time to go back and investigate.

The next twenty-four hours flew by quickly and it was shortly after two o'clock when Kathy dropped the twins at the Jefferson house. The leader's car was parked out front.

"I'd like to say hello to Mrs. Jefferson before you all take off for the wilds of

New Mexico," Kathy said, switching off the ignition.

The children led the way up the sidewalk, suddenly aware of a little girl watching them from inside the doorway.

"Are you a Camp Fire girl?" Flossie asked as the entrance swung open.

"Mm-hmm. My name's Ginny Parsons."

"Hi, I'm Flossie Bobbsey," the little twin said, then introduced the others.

As they stepped inside, they noticed that the left sleeve of Ginny's blouse was tucked inside her jeans.

"I'll bet you never thought you'd meet a real one-armed bandit." Ginny grinned, swinging back her thick brown hair.

"Are you a bandit?" Freddie asked.

"No," the girl said and laughed, "but I could be. I can do almost anything with one hand."

"So can I," Flossie giggled, sticking

her own left hand in her pocket. She tried to do a cartwheel but tumbled off balance, nearly knocking into Millie Jefferson as she came downstairs.

"Oops. Don't hurt yourself," the woman said, catching Flossie's hand.

"Excuse me," Flossie said sheepishly. "I was just trying to—"

"Show off for Ginny," Nan replied while Kathy gave the club leader the children's permission slip.

"Have fun," Kathy told the twins as she left. "See you on Sunday! Tony and I will pick you up from camp so Mrs. Jefferson won't have to drive you back."

Even though they were all curious to know more about Ginny's handicap, it was only Flossie who raised the question.

"Why do you only have one arm, Ginny?" she asked when they were in the Jefferson station wagon and leading a small caravan of cars northward.

"I was in a bad accident," the girl replied. "But it could've been worse. I could've lost both arms, and then I wouldn't have been able to hold my kitten or eat or put on my clothes or anything."

"Well, speaking of doing things," Millie Jefferson interrupted brightly, "we're going to make up a caper chart. That's a list of who's going to do all the chores at camp over the next two days."

"I can't wait to cook this time," Ginny said, explaining to the twins that everyone would take turns at different assignments. "Cleaning up stuff isn't so great," she admitted, "but building a campfire sure is!"

The children were eager to pitch in right away when the cars pulled into camp. Everything was quickly unloaded, then the Camp Fire members and visitors gathered in front of the dining-hall porch. Mrs. Jefferson and her assistant leader, Tammy, raised their hands for silence.

"I have an important introduction to make," Mrs. Jefferson said to the campers. She motioned the Bobbseys to step forward and announced their names. "They will probably be asking you a lot of questions."

"How come?" a little girl asked.

"Because they're detectives and they're trying to solve the case of our missing bicycles."

The twins kept smiling but secretly wished Mrs. Jefferson hadn't made such a big deal about their plans. Before she could say anything else, though, one of the younger boys held up his hand with great eagerness.

"Yes, Christopher?" the woman asked.

"There's no more case to solve," he said.

"I don't understand. What do you mean?"

"Just that. There's no more mystery. We're going to get our bicycles back!"

The Bobbseys gaped at him, completely flabbergasted.

·4·

Suspicions

As the Bobbseys stared open-mouthed at Christopher, he waved a newspaper clipping that appeared to be an advertisement of some sort.

"What's that?" Flossie inquired, running toward the boy.

"It's an ad for used bikes," he said.

"So?"

"Well, if this place buys used bikes, and the thieves read this ad, I'll bet they'll try to sell the stolen bicycles to this shop."

"Good reasoning," Bert remarked as he and Nan stood next to Christopher.

"I wonder if the ad was placed by Mr. Staley."

"Oh, boy," Nan said. "If the thieves try to sell their stolen goods to Mr. Staley, he'll recognize the bikes that belong to him for sure!"

"Exactly," her brother agreed. "We ought to call Mr. Staley right away. Is there a telephone that I can use, Mrs. Jefferson?"

"There certainly is," she said, excusing herself from the group to lead Bert to the camp office. "When you're finished, come back to the dining hall, okay?"

"Okay," the boy replied as he started to dial the number. The phone rang only once before the owner answered it. "Mr. Staley, is that you?" Bert asked.

"Tom Staley, at your service."

"Well, sir, I'm Bert Bobbsey—"

"Oh, yes. I heard about you Bobbsey children," the frail voice answered. "You're trying to help Narosonia find the stolen bicycles, aren't you?"

"Why, yes, but how did you know?" the young detective asked in astonishment, prompting a soft chuckle at the other end of the line.

"Albuquerque may be a big town, but the news travels pretty fast," the shop-owner answered. "Actually, Narosonia called me about the ad in the paper. She said some of the parents were thinking of getting together to buy replacements. But I told her to wait a little longer, be patient, if you know what I mean, and maybe the stolen ones would show up eventually." He paused with a deep sigh. "Between you and me, son, I think Narosonia is just trying to figure out a way to make up for my loss. And I just won't let her do it. My store isn't going to close up merely because a few bikes were taken."

"No one's tried to sell any of them back to you?" Bert asked.

"Sell me back my own bikes? Not so

far. But don't you worry your little head about it. If someone tries to, you won't need to set a fire under my toes. I'll call the police right away," he replied, still laughing as the young detective said good-bye.

When Bert told the other twins what he had learned, Freddie's face lit up in a big, happy grin. "So we have to keep working on the mystery, right?" he piped up.

"Right," Nan replied. "Meanwhile, though, we'd better unpack our stuff and get ready for a trust walk."

"What's a trust walk?" Bert asked in bewilderment.

"You'll see," his sister said. Her eyes twinkled as she darted to the girls' cabin.

"Come on, Freddie," Bert said, turnng in the opposite direction. "See you later, Floss."

But the little girl had already begun to chase after Nan. In no more than thirty minutes, they were all gath-

ered with the Camp Fire members at
the edge of a hilly clearing.

"Is everybody here?" Mrs. Jefferson
called out. She did a quick head count,
then passed out an equal number of
blindfolds. "Everyone pick a partner,"
she said, causing an excited murmur
among her eager listeners. They qui-
eted down the minute she started to
give instructions.

"We're going to take a walk two by
two," the woman said, "and each of you
is going to take a turn wearing a
blindfold."

"This sounds spooky," Flossie con-
fided to Ginny Parsons, who was her
teammate.

"Now hold your friend's hand or el-
bow," Mrs. Jefferson continued, "and
whoever gets to wear the blindfold first,
let your partner lead you. Then, leaders,
it will be up to you to ask if your
blindfolded pal can tell where you're
going. Ask if you're walking uphill or

down, for instance. Are you in the shade or are you in the sun? Think of other questions, too. Why don't you ask for a description of a tree or a certain kind of bird?"

"How long do we have?" one of the children called out.

"Oh," the leader pondered, "I'd say no more than ten minutes. Now, everybody, be careful where you walk. Stay on the footpaths at all times."

All the children, including the twins, took off in separate directions. Nan and Bert had paired up with two campers from their cabins while Freddie joined up with another boy, leaving Flossie and Ginny to head for a thicket of small trees.

"Where are we going?" Flossie asked, unable to see anything through the cloth covering her eyes.

Ginny laughed as she held the little girl's hand tightly. "That's what I'm supposed to ask you," she said, leading her friend deeper into the pine woods.

"Well, I just felt some leaves tickle my legs," Flossie reported, "and I smell Christmas trees, too, so I guess we're in the middle of lots of pine trees and bushes."

"That's right," Ginny answered. Suddenly, however, she noticed a piece of paper fluttering in a branch overhead. "Hmm," she said and stopped walking.

"What's wrong?" her companion asked.

Ginny did not respond right away, causing the Bobbsey girl to slip off her blindfold. "Look up there," Ginny said. "It's a piece of paper! I wonder where it came from and how it got into the tree. I'm going to get it."

"But you'll hurt yourself," Flossie protested.

"Me? Never. I told you I can do anything I want to. Now just stay put, all right?"

Instantly, the girl grabbed the gnarled

trunk with her right hand. She pulled herself up until her feet were on a knob of bark well off the ground, then reached for a low-hanging, spindly branch.

Flossie, meanwhile, stepped closer, biting her lower lip nervously as she watched the one-armed girl climb toward the second branch where the paper was caught. Now it was only a few inches away from Ginny's fingers. Suddenly, she slipped, and before Flossie could scream or move out of the way, the girl fell on top of her!

"Oh!" Ginny cried, as she rolled over the little twin, landing on a soft patch of dirt.

Flossie instantly felt a sharp pain streak through her left arm and she fought back tears.

"Oh—Ginny—oh, it hurts," she said as her companion crawled toward her.

"Don't move," Ginny ordered. "I'll get help right away."

She disappeared toward the clearing. A few minutes later, she returned with Mrs. Jefferson and the older Bobbsey twins.

"What happened?" Nan asked, darting toward her sister.

"I fell," Flossie cried, "and I hurt my arm."

"It's all my fault," Ginny said. "I was trying to show off how I could climb that tree. There's a piece of paper stuck in the branches—"

She pointed upward, but to her surprise the paper was gone.

"Is this it?" Bert asked, seeing it on the ground a few yards away. "It must've come down when you fell."

Ginny nodded while the boy glanced quickly at the paper. "It's an order form for 2,000 envelopes," he said, "from a printing outfit. But the address is torn off. All that's left is 'rd Printing,' and underneath, 'Road, Santa Fe, New Mexico 87501'."

Bert turned the form over and noticed some pencil marks on the other side. "Hm. '270° W,' it says. I wonder what it means."

"I have no idea," Nan commented.

Bert put the paper in his pocket while the club leader bent to examine Flossie's arm.

"It's not broken," she said.

"Are you sure?" Nan asked anxiously.

"Yes, dear. I'm a nurse," the woman replied, "and I'll have her fixed up in no time. It's just a sprain."

She lifted the child and whispered something that made her giggle, then carried her to a small infirmary on the camping grounds. When the little girl emerged at last with her arm in a sling, there was a hint of puffiness around her eyes, but she was smiling.

"I'm okay," Flossie told the other campers who were gathered outside to greet her.

Ginny instantly raced forward. "Are

you really all right?" she asked.

"Of course, I am," the young twin answered. "Now *we* look like twins!" she exclaimed, which made Ginny laugh.

"Tell you what. I'll teach you to catch a ball with one hand," the girl offered.

"You will?" Flossie said. But feeling a slight twinge in her bruised arm, she winced. "Maybe we ought to play later—or tomorrow."

"I think you ought to rest, young lady," Mrs. Jefferson suggested, and the other twins nodded their approval.

Nan immediately took her sister's good hand and led her to their cabin, leaving Bert and Freddie by themselves.

"I was going to throw this in the litter basket," Bert confessed, showing his brother the intriguing pencil marks. "It seems to me this is a compass reading. Now, how did it get up in that tree Ginny fell out of?"

"Somebody must have put it there,

Bert," Freddie answered quickly.

"Or, more likely, it fell out of something."

"You mean, like a helicopter or a balloon?"

Bert nodded, thoughtfully studying the paper. But Freddie grew restless with his brother's silence and walked away to start asking the campers about the bicycle thefts.

"Did you ever see anyone watching you while you were up here or at the Camp Fire office in Albuquerque?" the little detective inquired.

"Do you mean the day the bikes were stolen or before then?" a girl named Lydia replied.

"Either."

"No, but come to think of it," Christopher put in, "I did see somebody once."

"Well, what was he doing that made him seem suspicious?" Bert joined in.

"He was peeling a big potato!" the

other boy declared, bringing a round of laughter from his listeners.

Even Bert chuckled. "That's not a crime," he declared.

"True, but peeling and watching Mrs. Spatz and the rest of us at the same time sure is."

"What'd he look like?" Freddie asked.

"His most outstanding feature was his long hair. It was sort of greasy."

"When did you see this man?"

"About a week ago."

"What color was his hair?" Bert asked.

"I'm not sure," Christopher admitted.

"Was he with anyone else?"

"I don't know. I saw him get into a truck, but I don't remember seeing anyone else in it."

"Christopher," Lydia said thoughtfully, "where was I when you saw the guy with the potato?"

"I don't know—probably talking with

your girl friends," he answered.

No one else, however, had seen the greasy-haired character either. Nan, who had raced back to join the end of the discussion, later told Bert and Freddie that she was very puzzled.

"I wonder why nobody else saw the guy with the potato," she said.

"Maybe nobody else is as observant as Christopher," Bert said.

"Or has such an imagination!" Freddie exclaimed as if he knew something the other twins didn't.

On the Bluebird Trail

"What's wrong with Christopher's imagination?" Nan asked Freddie.

"Well, I saw him listening at the office door when Bert called the bicycle shop," the young detective reported.

"You did?" Bert said, surprised.

"Yes," Freddie replied, "and it seems to me he was awfully eager to tell us there was no more mystery to solve a few minutes ago."

"So maybe Christopher wants to play detective, too," Nan remarked.

"And he's hoping to solve the mystery before we do," her older brother said.

"Of course, I wouldn't blame him since one of the missing bikes belongs to him."

"But why would he make up a story about seeing a greasy-haired guy peeling a potato?" Bert inquired.

"I don't know. Maybe he didn't make it up," Nan said. "Maybe he really did see him."

"That's true," Freddie added. "I guess I jumped to a conclusion. A good detective shouldn't do that."

There was no time left to discuss the mystery any further, however, since everyone had been called to a big picnic table on which lay several pre-cut pieces of lumber and a variety of nails, along with some tools.

"What are we going to make?" Freddie asked Mrs. Jefferson as the campers gathered around her.

"Bluebird nesting boxes," she answered. Then, after a moment, she added, "Camp Fire has started a project to save the bluebirds from extinction."

"Are they all going to die?" the little boy asked.

"Well, we're going to try very hard to keep that from happening," the woman replied. "What they need most is a place to nest and raise their young."

"But there are so many trees for them to live in," Freddie continued. "Why don't they use them?"

Mrs. Jefferson smiled, patting the twin affectionately under his chin. "I'm sure they'd like to," she said, "but un-

Constructing the Bluebird Box

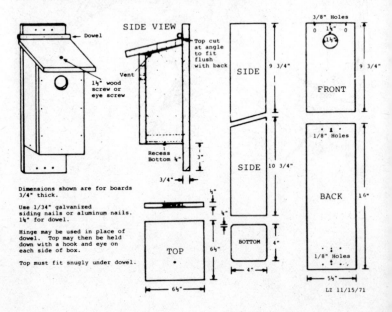

fortunately the English sparrows and European starlings have beaten the poor bluebirds to it. That's why we have to build them something with very specific dimensions."

As she showed the children how to construct their own bluebird boxes, she explained that a trail of boxes should always be set up in an open, unobstructed area.

"Bluebirds won't nest in the woods or deep shade. They like lots of sunlight," Mrs. Jefferson added. "The best spot would be where there are only scattered trees. A field like the one a few miles up the road would be perfect. I spoke to the owner of the ranch the other day and got permission for us to put up our own bluebird trail. His caretaker, Mr. Marshall, will help us."

"Oh, that sounds super!" Ginny Parsons exclaimed.

Then the campers lapsed into silence, concentrating eagerly on their work. By the time they finished, the sunlight had started to fade.

"The caper chart's tacked up on the tree outside the dining hall," Mrs. Jefferson announced, "so check your assignments before you wash up for dinner."

The twins laid their completed bluebird boxes next to the others in a big carton, then hurried to the tree. On it were the names of all the campers along with a colorful symbol for each one. Freddie chuckled when he saw his.

"I'm a squirrel," he said.

"That must mean you're a little nutty," Nan teased, noting that the boy had been assigned to help set the dinner table.

She and Bert, on the other hand, had been chosen to build the campfire later that evening.

"Lucky you," Ginny said to Nan with a big grin on her face. "Everybody loves to build the campfire. I did it last time."

"I can't wait!" Nan exclaimed happily. Together they dashed toward their cabin.

They eagerly told Flossie about the next day's plan to put up a trail of bluebird boxes, but she reacted without much enthusiasm.

"Don't you feel well, Floss?" Nan asked.

"I'm okay—I guess."

But the little girl could not ignore the slight ache in her arm for the rest of the evening. She picked at the delicious chicken supper and listened half-heartedly to the round of songs that the other children sang around the crackling fire.

Ginny, in the meantime, had moved closer to Flossie. "Does your arm bother you a whole lot?" she inquired.

"Not a lot."

"But enough, I'll bet," Ginny said. "Mine bothers me, too, sometimes."

"It does?" Flossie asked in amazement. She glanced at the girl's half-empty sleeve.

"I know it sounds strange, but it's true," Ginny went on. "Sometimes it feels as if my arm is still there. Isn't that silly? You know, I really am sorry about what happened today."

"It's all right."

"No, it isn't."

The downhearted expression on Ginny's face prompted Flossie to smile. "Will you play ball with me before we leave?" she asked.

"Sure. But do you trust me to teach you how to catch with one hand?" Ginny answered.

"Mm-hmm," the little girl said confidently.

By the next morning, Flossie felt much better. The ache in her arm had almost disappeared, and without any help, she dressed herself and hurried after the other campers who piled into an old van.

"Where are the bluebird boxes?" Mrs. Jefferson called before stepping into the driver's seat next to her assistant, Tammy.

Then she noticed the big carton on the porch of the dining hall and sent two of the children to pick it up.

"We can't forget *them*," Flossie said to her sister as the engine began to drone.

"Is everybody set?" the club leader asked, backing the van down the gravel road at last.

Her small passengers laughed and talked all the way to the clearing that Mrs. Jefferson had told them about. Upon reaching a grove of trees that stood in single file along the road, she swung the van to the side and halted. The children scrambled out quickly and unloaded the bluebird boxes.

"We're going to put them up every hundred yards or so in a circle," Mrs. Jefferson instructed. "I brought some wooden posts and metal collars to attach under the boxes."

"What are those for?" Nan inquired.

"To help protect the birds from predators like the coyote and fox," Tammy replied. "Now let's get going."

Mr. Marshall, the caretaker of the ranch, had already dug deep holes in the ground and put up the posts. He made sure that each one was firmly set, then Mrs. Jefferson signaled the children to begin mounting the boxes. The older twins busied themselves at one end of the circle while the younger ones ran to the other end.

"Hey, Flossie!" Freddie exclaimed. "Look at those! His chubby fingers motioned to a line of fresh tire marks that cut along the edge of the tall grass and vanished into the woods. "Come on!" he shouted eagerly.

"But what about the bluebird boxes?" the little girl asked.

"Come on. This'll only take a minute," the boy insisted.

He sped toward the rutted road that bordered the clearing and waved Flossie to follow. She did so reluctantly, but paused before slipping into the shade of the trees. Nan and Bert caught sight of her and called out. Their voices, however, went unheard as Freddie urged her on.

Deeper and deeper the young twins pushed into the forest, trailing after the tire marks on the wide dirt path until they came to a wooden shed. There was no sign of a car anywhere.

"Be careful," Flossie warned her brother. "Someone might be in there!" But he had already flung open the door.

"Come here," he said, stepping inside and drawing the small girl after him. "It's empty."

"No, it isn't," Flossie responded,

picking up a small tube-shaped bag with tabs that snapped at each end. "It's a bike pack."

"Hmm. I wonder how it got there," Freddie said.

"Somebody must've been bike riding in the woods," Flossie replied.

She opened the thin zipper that ran along the length of the bag and poked her hand in. "Look, Freddie! Here's a newspaper clipping!" she said excitedly.

"Yeah, and it's about bikes that were stolen from Santa Fe!" the boy exclaimed.

He took the bag out of Flossie's hands, suddenly aware of the two large figures standing in the doorway. They leaped toward the children, pouncing on them before they could run away!

"Oh, no!" the Bobbsey twins cried out helplessly.

·6·

Santa Fe Sleuths

Freddie clung to the bike pack, kicking the man who tried dragging him toward the door.

"Why, you little—" the man rasped at the boy while his companion clapped a hand over Flossie's mouth and pulled her outside.

Suddenly, the sound of footsteps running through the woods seemed to panic the men. They shoved the twins aside.

"Let's get out of here!" one of the abductors exclaimed, dashing behind the shed.

Freddie and Flossie ran after them, catching a glimpse of stringy blond hair before the men leaped into a truck and shot off down another path.

"Those are the two who work with Ryan Michaels!" Freddie cried, his voice attracting the ears of Bert, Nan, and the few campers who hurried toward the shed.

"What's going on?" Nan asked breathlessly.

"We followed the tire marks," Bert said, "and just before we got here, we heard you scream."

"They would've kidnapped us if you hadn't come after us," Flossie blurted.

"Who would have?"

"Those two men—the ones who were with Ryan Michaels the other day! They jumped us in the shed!" Freddie explained. "I think they came for this!" He held out the bike pack for Bert to look at.

"There's a newspaper clipping inside," Flossie noted, prompting the older boy to look for it right away.

His eyes widened as he and Nan read the story. "According to this, somebody has been stealing bicycles around Santa Fe and Pecos, and some kids have started a search party," Bert said. "The girl who's in charge is Amanda Friedman. She's from Pecos."

"And that's where those two stringy-haired men said they wanted to go," Freddie pointed out.

As he spoke, Bert began to examine the pack more thoroughly. He found a tiny label glued inside the flap.

"Guess what?" he said. "This belongs to Randall Friedman." He glanced at the newspaper again. "He must be Amanda's brother," Bert added.

"We'd better go see them tomorrow," Flossie suggested.

"Most definitely," Nan replied as the group headed back to the clearing.

"You know what? I bet those men used that shed to store bicycles. Why else would they have come to pick up this bike pack?" Bert said. "The only reason I can think of is to remove the last bit of evidence."

"The snaps on the pack must've opened when they dumped the bikes in the truck," Nan said, "and the men probably noticed later that the pack was missing."

"And that's when they came back to the shed and found us!" Flossie exclaimed.

"Exactly," her sister said.

The foursome hurried over to Mrs. Jefferson, quickly telling her what had just happened.

"We'd better go right back to camp and call the police," she decided.

"But we haven't finished setting up the bluebird trail," Nan commented. "Those men are gone now, anyway, and I don't think the police could catch them even if we phoned in a report this very minute."

The woman hesitated before she finally nodded. Nevertheless, she pressed the campers to complete their work. "And no more trips into the woods, all right?" she said, glancing sternly at the young twins.

When the group returned to camp at last, she put a call in to the nearest police station and let Freddie and Flossie describe the men over the phone.

"Did you see their license plate?" the lieutenant asked.

"No, sir," Freddie replied. "The truck left too fast, but we're pretty sure it belongs to a man named Ryan Michaels."

"And where's he from?"

The little boy explained how they had met the balloonist in Albuquerque. "But I don't know if he lives there. He could be from Santa Fe or Pecos or even from somewhere else," Freddie said.

The conversation ended shortly and the young detective related it to the other twins.

"Now I know why Ryan was acting so

strangely when he was forced to land on the Leonards' property," Nan said. "No wonder he refused to go to the hospital, and when we mentioned the rip in his balloon, he told us to mind our own business."

"Sure, he didn't want the police to get involved and ask him questions," Bert said.

"And remember how he didn't want to stay for tea?" Flossie added. "That's because he had something to hide and didn't want to talk to us."

"If I only knew what he was up to on that footpath the night we took the tram up the mountain," Bert said. "Maybe the thieves have another hide-out there in the woods just like the shed we found."

The twins' excitement mounted as they pieced together their latest clues, and they were eager to tell the Leonards all about them.

The next day, when they were together again, they discussed their new plan.

"We were wondering if you'd mind taking us to Pecos," Nan asked Kathy and Tony. "It's really important for us to talk to Amanda and Randall Friedman."

"Well, it's fine with me," Kathy said cheerfully. She murmured under her breath to her husband, "Mary told me they wouldn't give up once they got on a hot trail."

"And it's hot, all right!" Nan said, laughing as she overheard the remark.

The visitors then said good-bye to the campers. "If we get any more leads, we'll call you!" Christopher shouted while Ginny huddled next to the Leonards' car.

"I hope your arm gets better real soon," she told Flossie.

"Oh, it will. It feels better already. I'm just sorry we didn't have time to play."

Promising to keep in touch with the

girl, the twins waved again and settled back in their seats. By now the temperature had climbed several degrees but the mountain breeze felt cool against their faces as they rode toward the highway; Kathy turned the conversation to the broad sweep of flatland that soon surrounded them.

"New Mexico must look very different from Lakeport," she said.

"Oh, it does," Flossie answered. "We don't have any desert at all. But I'd sure like to get some."

"Well, maybe we can send a bagful of sand and tumbleweed home with you." The young woman laughed.

"Could you put in a yucca, too, like the ones you have in your front yard?" Nan said, giggling.

"Just pick any one you want," Tony said.

Despite the monotony of the road, which carried little traffic, the time seemed to fly, and the travelers soon found themselves climbing through thick, green countryside. There were only a few old buildings scattered along the way. Among them was a house, but its vacant appearance indicated that no one, including the Friedmans, had occupied it recently.

"We'll have to ask someone where they live," Nan said, prompting Mr. Leonard to pull into a parking lot of a small button factory called THE HANDS WORK. Its friendly houselike exterior was so appealing, it seemed to invite visitors.

"May I help you?" the young woman asked as the twins stepped inside. She was painting flowers on a small, delicate clay button.

"We hope so," Flossie said, watching a man behind the woman put a tray of other buttons inside a kiln. "We're the Bobbsey twins and we're looking for a girl named Amanda Friedman. Do you know her?"

"We sure do. Pecos isn't a very big place, and everybody who lives here knows just about everybody else," the buttonmaker replied. She smiled under a mane of shiny dark hair. "But I'll have to check with the Friedmans before I give you their address. Ever since the story about Amanda appeared in the newspaper, they've been getting some pretty weird phone calls and visitors."

"We're not weirdos," Freddie stated indignantly.

"I didn't say that you were. Still, I'd better make sure it's all right to send you over there."

The comment caused an eyeroll between the older children, while Flossie whispered to her brother, "I guess they haven't heard about the Bobbsey detective team around here," she said.

But when the young woman returned, she was laughing. "Oh—I'm really sorry," she apologized. "The minute I mentioned your names, Amanda got all

excited. She told me about the mysteries you've solved and how she and
her brother want to be detectives, too."

As she said this, she drew a little map
of the road they were on, showing a
turn-off that led to the Friedmans'
ranch.

"Thanks a lot!" the children exclaimed
and bounced out the door to the car.

The ride to the ranch proved as unex-
pected and spectacular as everything
else they had seen in New Mexico. The
road coiled between mountains of cot-
tonwood and tall ponderosa pines, following the curve of the winding river
below.

Then, suddenly, Flossie spotted the
stone entrance that was marked on the
map. "That's it!" she exclaimed, seeing
two children running up the driveway.

Mr. Leonard stopped the car and
greeted the pretty little girl with soft
brown hair and her younger brother
who wore an impish grin on his face.

"Hi!" they called out happily when the twins leaped out of the car, bringing the Leonards behind them.

"We read about you in the newspaper," Nan told Amanda who blushed in embarrassment.

"Is that why you came here?" the girl asked. "To help us find our bicycles?"

"Sure it is," Randall Friedman said, taking in a deep breath. "Now we'll have the best search party ever!"

"Well," Bert interrupted, "we've already started looking for some missing bikes that were stolen from a camp not far from here."

"And don't forget about Mr. Staley's bikes," Nan reminded him. "They were taken from the Camp Fire office in Albuquerque."

"Maybe they were all taken by the same thief," Amanda said quickly.

"Got any clues yet?" Randall inquired.

"A few," Flossie said while Bert

handed over the bike pack.

"Where'd you find this?" he asked, jumping with excitement.

"In a shed in the woods," Freddie answered, telling about the clearing and the tire marks.

"The Bobbseys were almost kidnapped," Kathy Leonard said.

"Really?" Amanda gasped.

The younger twins nodded. "But *almost* doesn't count," Freddie said. "We got a look at the men, though, and we know who they are."

"Who?" Randall questioned.

"Two men who work with a balloonist named Ryan Michaels. We think he's in it, too. All we have to do is prove it."

"Tell us about the thefts in Santa Fe," Bert asked the Friedman children.

"Were the bikes taken all at once or were they stolen at different times?" Nan added.

"Different times," Amanda replied.

"Five of them disappeared first, then another six."

"The first bunch was parked outside the weaving center on Canyon Road," Randall explained. "That's in the downtown part of Santa Fe. The rest were up near the cave. We'll show it to you."

Just then, Mr. and Mrs. Friedman, a young, good-looking couple in jeans and Western-style shirts, emerged from the lower field. After a round of introductions, Randall asked if he and Amanda could take the twins to the cave up the road.

"On one condition only," Mrs. Friedman said with firmness, "that you don't stay up there too long."

"We won't," Amanda promised. "Let's go, everybody!" She raced up the driveway, leading the other children onto the road. They sprinted ahead for some distance before the girl finally

stopped, breathless, and pointed to a steep, gravel slope that ended in a forbidding, black hole in the rocky mountain.

"That's the cave," she said, "and that's where our bicycles were parked."

Nan observed how close the road was to the slope. "The thieves obviously pulled up their truck and snitched the bikes while you were inside the cave," she said.

"Precisely," Amanda said.

At the same time, they all noticed a big hot-air balloon rising over the treetops. It had bluebirds all around it!

"That's Ryan's balloon!" Bert exclaimed, feeling a rush of excitement.

· 7 ·

Pecos Prisoners?

As the large balloon flew behind the trees, it dipped out of sight. But the children kept their eyes fastened on the milky-blue sky, waiting for it to reappear.

"I think it's headed for the river!" Randall declared. "Come on, hurry!"

Instantly, the group ran after him. To their surprise, though, the balloon began to veer in another direction. It crossed under the clouds, then sank below other trees.

"What'll we do?" Amanda asked the others.

"Is there a field up in those hills?" Bert questioned.

"I don't know. Maybe."

"Well, if there isn't, then I wonder how Ryan plans to make a landing," Nan said. "We'd better find out."

The children followed the road for another mile, but there was no sign of the balloon.

"He must've landed farther away than we realized," Bert said at last. "Amanda, is there another road or footpath that goes up past those trees?" He pointed to a bank of aspens on the right.

"I don't know about a road, but there is a path somewhere not far from here."

She and her brother led the way to a break in the trees, which indicated the beginning of a dirt path. For more than fifteen minutes, the group trekked through the sweet-smelling woods that finally opened on a wide field.

"This is the biggest meadow I've ever seen," Bert commented just before his eyes settled on the half-empty balloon bobbing in the tall grass. "There it is!" he exclaimed, dashing ahead of the others. "And the pilot's gone!"

Except for Freddie and Randall, the rest of the children followed. But as they drew closer, they realized that two of their companions were missing!

"Where are they?" Flossie cried.

A few minutes earlier, Freddie and Randall had seen Ryan's dog Lady run into the woods. She was running after the balloonist who seemed to be in a big hurry.

"Let's go after them," Randall suggested.

"Maybe we ought to tell the others first," Freddie started to say, but he realized that they'd lose time.

Instead, the two children sped into the forest. They were certain that the shade of the trees and the soft brown earth would hide their movements well.

But just as they spied the balloon truck at the edge of a dirt clearing, two figures plunged forward. In a flash, they dropped sacks over the boys' heads, muffling their cries. Then they carried their captives to the truck.

"Help!" Freddie screamed, but it did no good. They were too far away from the others to be heard. Discouraged, the little boy sank limply between Randall and someone else who seemed to be much bigger than either of them.

The other children, meanwhile, grew frantic when they realized that the boys had vanished.

"Now what?" Amanda asked.

"Maybe Ryan kidnapped them," Nan said, frowning grimly.

Her older brother did not respond to the comment. He called out the boys' names and suggested that everybody split up for the search. "Nan, you check the area to the right. Amanda, you and

Flossie try the left. I'll scout around here."

Nan, however, was the only one who found a series of footprints along the trail of pine trees. She tracked them to the edge of the forest. There, to her astonishment, she discovered a dirt road and wheel marks in the dust.

"Oh!" she cried aloud as she spotted a small Camp Fire insignia shining in the sunlight.

"That's the clip from Freddie's bolo tie!" she gasped, then raced back to the balloon site.

"We'd better call the police," Bert said when he saw the insignia.

Without wasting another second, the children sped across the field and through the trees to the road. They ran as fast as they could, not stopping once to catch their breath until they reached the ranch.

Amanda burst into the house. "Randall's gone!" she cried out. "He and

Freddie have been kidnapped!"

"What?" her mother said incredulously, but the other children confirmed the story.

"This is terrible! Roger, we must do something!" Mrs. Friedman exclaimed.

Her husband had already started dialing a number for the police while the twins told the Leonards that they were sure the captives had been taken away in the balloon truck.

"Maybe we can catch it," Tony Leonard said.

"You go ahead. I'll stay here with Amanda and her parents," Kathy said, "in case the police need more information."

But the rest of her statement went unheard as the twins jumped into the station wagon and Tony soared onto the road.

"Maybe the gasoline attendant here saw the truck," Bert suggested when a

service station came into view near the
sign for Santa Fe.

"We'll ask him," Tony agreed and
stopped the car.

"Hmm," the man mumbled upon
hearing the question. "I don't reckon
too many trucks go past with a balloon
on it. Let me make a call." He strode
into his small glass-fronted office and
picked up the phone.

"I wonder who he's talking to," Nan
said, echoing everyone else's thoughts.

When the attendant finally returned,
he was smiling, obviously satisfied. "I
gave my friend Sam Butler a buzz," he
revealed. "He's an old codger like me.
Lives up the street and sits by his window most of the day. Nothing much
slips past his eyes, let me tell you."

"Did he see the truck?" Nan pressed
him.

"Yep. He says he did. A white one
with a big balloon painted on the side,

just like the one you described."

"Which way was it going?" Tony inquired.

"Straight down this road."

"Did Mr. Butler tell you anything else about the truck?" Nan questioned.

"Not a thing. Why? Were you planning to catch a ride in that contraption?" the man asked with a look of curiosity.

"No, sir. We're trying to catch kidnappers," Bert said flatly. "So if that truck should pass by again, tell Mr. Butler to call the police. Okay?"

The man was so dumbstruck by the boy's request that he didn't even reply and watched the car swing out of the station.

Suddenly, after passing acres of fenced-in property, Flossie saw a collie running playfully near an entrance marked Pecos National Monument.

"That's Lady!" she exclaimed.

"You're right, Flossie!" Nan and Bert chimed in.

"Maybe the truck went in there," Tony remarked.

"Or maybe the dog just jumped out," Flossie said.

"Well, I doubt that the dog would do that if the truck was moving quickly. It must've slowed down here," Mr. Leonard said, turning into the entrance.

"But why would the kidnappers bring the kids here?" Bert asked. "It's a public place and someone would be bound to see them."

"I don't see anyone around, though," Nan replied, looking around at the pueblo ruins and remains of the ancient Franciscan mission. "Maybe it's closed today. Besides, the collie's here. So Ryan could be, too."

As she spoke, the dog yelped and leaped after the car, following it to a parking space near a small adobe building marked VISITOR CENTER. Despite the dog's insistent barking, they went inside. There was only one person on the premises, and she was seated behind a counter filled with postcards.

"Excuse us," Nan said, causing the woman to look up from the book she was reading. "Did you happen to see a truck pull in a little while ago?"

"I couldn't tell you. Unless somebody comes in here I really don't pay much attention," she said.

Frustrated, the children studied the postcards carefully. Among them were pictures of the small adobe rooms, called *kivas*, that lay deep within the ruins.

"Maybe Freddie and Randall are in one of them," Nan whispered hopefully.

"And maybe Lady can tell us which one!" Bert added.

·8·

The Capture

Mr. Leonard and the twins walked out of the building, listening to the light movement of wind passing over the excavation site. Except for the sound of the breeze, their footsteps on the walkway, and the collie's barking, it was completely quiet.

"Show us where they are," Bert told the dog, bending to pet her. The animal lurched up the path away from him. "That's it," the boy said, "take us to Freddie and Randall."

The dog trotted past the long adobe brick wall that ran beyond one of the pueblos and stopped.

"You were right," Nan told her brother in a gleeful voice. They caught up to Lady, who was standing at the edge of a *kiva*. A small wooden ladder stood inside, which the twins scampered down quickly. To their chagrin, however, the room below was empty!

"I spoke too soon," Nan said, disappointed.

"We'll have to check the other *kivas*," Bert told her, leading the way back up.

Tony, in the meantime, had found something lying in the grass and was examining it. "Take a look at this," he said. "It's a pen."

Bert took it and turned it over. There was a small bluebird on one side of it.

"Maybe Ryan lost it," Nan offered. "Since his dog took us to this spot, perhaps he was here after all."

"Maybe we should explore the rest of the ruins," Bert suggested. "He could still be here."

The other children agreed. To save

time, everyone took a separate path, but when they all met again, they had found nothing of interest.

"Well, I'd like to drive up the road a little farther, if you don't mind," Tony Leonard said.

"We don't mind," Nan said, "but what about Lady?"

"We'll have to leave her here for the time being. I'm sure she'll be all right," he said.

The ride proved futile, however. There was no sign of the truck anywhere.

Sad and discouraged, they started toward the ranch once more.

Then, suddenly, Bert snapped his fingers. "I've got it!" he cried out.

"What?" Nan prodded him.

"Bluebirds! That's the key to everything!" he exclaimed.

"What are you talking about, Bert?" Flossie asked, puzzled.

"Bluebirds, that's what. They're all

over that balloon as big as life and I never gave them a second thought."

The boy detective dug into his pocket for the pen and the scrap of paper that Ginny had discovered in the tree at camp.

"It's a long shot, I know. But look at this again—'rd Printing,'" he said, pointing to the letters on the form.

"Maybe the rest of the word is Bluebird—Bluebird Printing."

"So?" Flossie asked.

"Don't you see? Ryan Michaels's balloon has bluebirds all over it. Suppose he owns the Bluebird Printing Company. This order for envelopes could have fallen out of his pocket while he was flying his balloon. That would also explain the pencil notation on the back—'270° West.' Maybe he didn't need the order form any more and used it to write on while he was up in the balloon!"

"That's possible," Nan said. "I'm sure

he must work, and he did say he only
flew his balloon for the fun of it. The
pen could be one of those gifts com-
panies sometimes give away to their
customers for advertising reasons. Instead of putting the company name on
the pen, Ryan put on a bluebird!"

"You've got it," Bert said, flashing a
grin.

"They probably use the truck for deliveries, for chasing the balloon, and for
stealing bicycles!" Flossie exclaimed.

"We'll have to find out the address of
the Bluebird Printing Company," Bert
declared. "It's too bad the name of the
street was ripped off the order form."

The children could barely contain
their excitement when they were in
the Friedmans' living room again and requested to see the telephone directory
for Santa Fe, explaining their theory to
Amanda and the adults.

"Here you are," Mr. Friedman said,
offering the thick book.

"Thanks," Nan said and leafed through the listings under B. "I found it!" she exclaimed a few moments later. "Bluebird Printing Company on Canyon Road."

"That's where the weaving center is!" Amanda cried.

Although a report had already been given to the police concerning the disappearance of the children, the lieutenant had no further news when he received the second call. Upon hearing the Bobbseys' discovery, he agreed to send several patrol cars to the Bluebird Company address in Santa Fe.

By the time the twin detectives and their friends reached Canyon Road, the police had already arrived.

"There it is!" Flossie exclaimed, pointing to the small stucco building that bore a handsomely printed sign in its window.

"You folks stay out here," one of the

officers advised the Leonards, unaware that Bert had ducked away from their car to the back of the building.

His eyes moved from the closed, dusty windows to a cellar door that looked fairly warped. If only he could get it to open!

Taking a deep breath, he tugged on the latch until it gave way and stepped inside.

The large basement room was filled with printing supplies and near the door stood a pile of wooden crates. Suddenly, the young detective heard a man's husky voice from a small room in the rear, and he darted behind the boxes.

"The cops are here! I just saw them through the window. Let's go!"

"What about the kids?" a second man sputtered.

"Forget about them. We may not even make it ourselves. Come on—move! We'll take the back door!"

Bert's mind buzzed with questions. What if the police weren't in position yet behind the building and the men managed to slip through their fingers?

I've got to stop them! the boy determined, hoping that the door he came through was the only way out for the men.

He heard footsteps advancing, then the pair stopped briefly before hurrying forward again. At that very instant, Bert knew what he had to do. He grabbed the top crate and shoved it in their path. Then he pushed another and another. As the crates slammed into each other, cans of ink flew in every direction, tripping the men and making them fall under the boxes.

One of them bellowed angrily at the boy, but Bert ignored him and called for help at the top of his lungs. In no time at all, several police officers burst into the cellar and dived for the stringy-haired thieves.

A minute later, the other Bobbseys rushed in after them. "Bert, are you all right?" his twin sister asked, stepping forward.

"Of course, I am," he said, pretending to be smug.

"Where are Freddie and Randall?" Flossie questioned.

She and the other children were scurrying past the overturned crates, peering anxiously into every shadow-filled corner. Then they heard a low, pitiful cry. It sounded muffled, almost distant. As their eyes rested on a door, they knew the sound had come from behind it.

"Oh!" Nan exclaimed as she pulled open the door.

In the small room beyond lay three bound figures: Freddie, Randall, and Ryan Michaels!

Quickly, the twins removed the gags that had been stuffed in the prisoners' mouths and released their bonds.

"Are you hurt?" Bert asked, helping the boys to their feet.

"No," Freddie said, "just thirsty."

Ryan, on the other hand, was rubbing the back of his head. "They knocked me out when I saw them pounce on these two up in the woods," he explained.

"They threw sacks over us," Randall said, indicating the heavy cloths on the floor. "We yelled for help but I guess you didn't hear us."

"No, we sure didn't," Nan said. "But when I found Freddie's Camp Fire insignia on the road next to the tire marks, I figured somebody took you away."

As they rejoined the policemen who had just finished handcuffing the prisoners, the two stringy-haired men glared at the Bobbseys and Ryan.

"We had a nice thing going, boss," one of them sneered.

"I'm sure you did. You could make deliveries for me and pick up bikes along the way," Ryan said. He turned to the children. "I happened to find a few bikes out in my back shed several days ago. The next thing I knew, there was a story in the paper about stolen bikes. I knew someone in my employ was responsible but I wasn't completely sure who it was, and before I made any accusations, the bikes disappeared. I wanted to solve things myself without police help so I could avoid bad publicity. It might have hurt my business."

"I saw you walking in the Sandia Mountains on the same day you landed in the Leonards' yard," Bert spoke up. "Were you looking for evidence?"

"More bikes, actually," Ryan confirmed. "I overheard one of the culprits talking about stashing them in a shed. Somewhere along the line, he also said something about the Sandias, so I figured the shed was there. But I never found it. Anyway, my friends obviously suspected that I was onto them. They cut my balloon and tampered with one of

the propane tanks, hoping to injure me
long enough to get rid of all the stolen
bikes and leave New Mexico. Right?"
He looked at the prisoners.

"I told you we should've skipped out
a long time ago," one of them growled at
the other. "But no, you didn't want to
give up anything. You even insisted—"

"Shut up!" the other man snapped
back.

Just then, several more officers
walked into the basement, pushing two
men ahead of them. "These fellows just
arrived. When they saw us, they tried to
run away. Does anybody know them?"
an officer asked.

"Yes," Ryan spoke up. "They work for
me."

"But they said they were policemen,"
Bert said.

The baffled officers stared at the boy
while his twin sister explained.

"They came to the Camp Fire office
in Albuquerque to follow up on the

bicycle thefts," Nan said. "Come to think of it, they did act sort of strangely."

"Now it's all starting to fit," Bert said. "The thieves must have seen us go to the Camp Fire office, and sent their spies in after us in a phony police car. No doubt they wanted to find out what we knew and what we were going to do about it. So they posed as police officers and asked a lot of questions."

One of the stringy-haired captives glared at the newcomers. "That was pretty stupid of you to walk right into the arms of the cops," he jeered.

"Well, you called us so we could all leave together," came the angry reply. "You didn't tell us the law was already in your backyard!"

Before another word could be spoken, handcuffs were put on the men and everyone went outside.

"It was a great little scheme," one of the prisoners muttered sadly.

"It's too bad the balloon flew out of control in Pecos," Flossie said. "Otherwise you might have gotten away with it."

"You can say that again," he hissed, "and too bad you squirts messed up everything!"

The little girl merely smiled and tried not to giggle as his face turned red. He grumbled in disgust, but the police pulled him and his companions toward a waiting car.

"Get in," one of the officers ordered gruffly.

"Just a minute, officer," Ryan requested. "I'd like to ask these men what happened to my dog!"

"Lady's safe and at the Pecos National Monument," Bert assured him, giving the bluebird pen to Ryan. "We found this, too."

"It must've fallen out of my pocket," the balloonist said, confused. "But I was probably unconscious at the time because I don't even remember being at the monument."

"We were, though," Randall told him.

"The men tried to dump us in one of the *kivas*."

"But when they took us off the truck, your dog jumped out and they couldn't get her back on. She wanted to stay with you," Freddie added.

"They were worried she'd bark and make a fuss, I guess, so they dragged us into the truck again," the other boy continued. "Naturally, Lady followed but they kicked her off."

The four prisoners, who were now seated in the backs of two cars, shot grim looks at the children.

"Sounds like your dog is a real lifesaver," Mr. Friedman said to Ryan.

"Not to mention the Bobbseys," the young man added. "I owe them a debt of gratitude on more than one account."

The Leonards and the Friedmans learned all the details of the capture later on. But it wasn't until the twins had made their report at headquarters that the lieutenant heard the whole story.

When they finished, his face broke into a big smile. "You know, you kids are pretty smart detectives," he complimented them. "When you're old enough, I'd like you to come work in Santa Fe."

"You mean it?" the younger twins said, brimming with enthusiasm.

"I certainly do."

"Lieutenant, believe me," Kathy Leonard said, "these children are dogged pursuers of justice—"

"And crooks!" Nan exclaimed. "Still, we didn't find the bikes."

"I think most of the missing bicycles will be retrieved," the lieutenant informed her. "The men told us to whom they were sold and where they hid the money. So we expect to get most of the bikes back."

The next morning, the twins were greeted with even more good news.

Their parents flew into Albuquerque, and they received a phone call from Mrs. Spatz, who invited them to a special celebration party.

"Can you come?" the council executive director asked.

"We sure can," Nan said. "But may we bring the rest of our Santa Fe detective team?"

"You may bring whomever you wish, my dear."

As plans developed for the evening at Millie Jefferson's home, the Bobbseys wondered if their next mystery would be as challenging as this one. They would find out soon when they stumbled on *Double Trouble*.

In the meantime, though, the party at Mrs. Jefferson's became the perfect ending to their trip west. Ginny Parsons had helped bake a special cake that was decorated with red, white, and blue icing—the colors of Camp Fire. In the center was a triangle with the word WOHELO printed around it.

"What does that mean, Ginny?" Flossie asked.

"It's a word made from the first letters of work, health, and love. Wohelo is our watchword at Camp Fire. And see where I wrote your name?"

The little Bobbsey girl found FLOSSIE printed at the end of the triangle.

"Flossie-lo," she said, laughing.

"Not lo. Love. We love all of you very much," Ginny said, smiling at the four twins.

"We do, too," Amanda added.

"Then here's to the best set of detectives this side of the Rio Grande!" Mrs. Spatz said, letting Nan cut the first slice of cake.

"Don't forget the Pecos River, too!" Randall exclaimed.

"But the real thanks still goes to Camp Fire," Bert declared, "because if you hadn't given Freddie that nice bolo tie, Mrs. Spatz, we might never have figured out the. mystery. So here's to Camp Fire!

THE BOBBSEY TWINS ® SERIES
by Laura Lee Hope

The Blue Poodle Mystery (#1)

Secret in the Pirate's Cave (#2)

The Dune Buggy Mystery (#3)

The Missing Pony Mystery (#4)

The Rose Parade Mystery (#5)

The Campfire Mystery (#6)

Double Trouble (#7)

Mystery of the Laughing Dinosaur (#8)

The Music Box Mystery (#9)

The Ghost in the Computer (#10)